Time for ^EARTH School, Dewey Dew

Written by
Leslie Staub

Illustrated by
Jeff Mack

Boyds Mills Press
An Imprint of Highlights
815 Church Street
Honesdale, Pennsylvania 18431

Printed in China
ISBN: 978-1-59078-958-2
Library of Congress Control Number: 2015946892

First edition
Design by Sara Gillingham Studio
Production by Sue Cole
The text of this book is set in Billy Serif, Brandon Printed,
Clarendon, School Script, and Sweater School.
The illustrations are done in pencil,
watercolor, and digital media.
10 9 8 7 6 5 4 3 2 1

To Kathy Brown with galaxies of love.
What on Earth would I do without you? —LS

For my friends, David, Diane, Mordicai,
and Shelley —JM

**Click-Clack Waddle-Waddle
Dot-Dot Dewey Dew** from
Planet Eight Hundred Seventy-Two Point Nine
did **not** want to go to school—

not on
SPACE STATION ZOOMALOT,

and definitely not at *Ms. Brightsun's School for Little Learners* on Planet Earth.

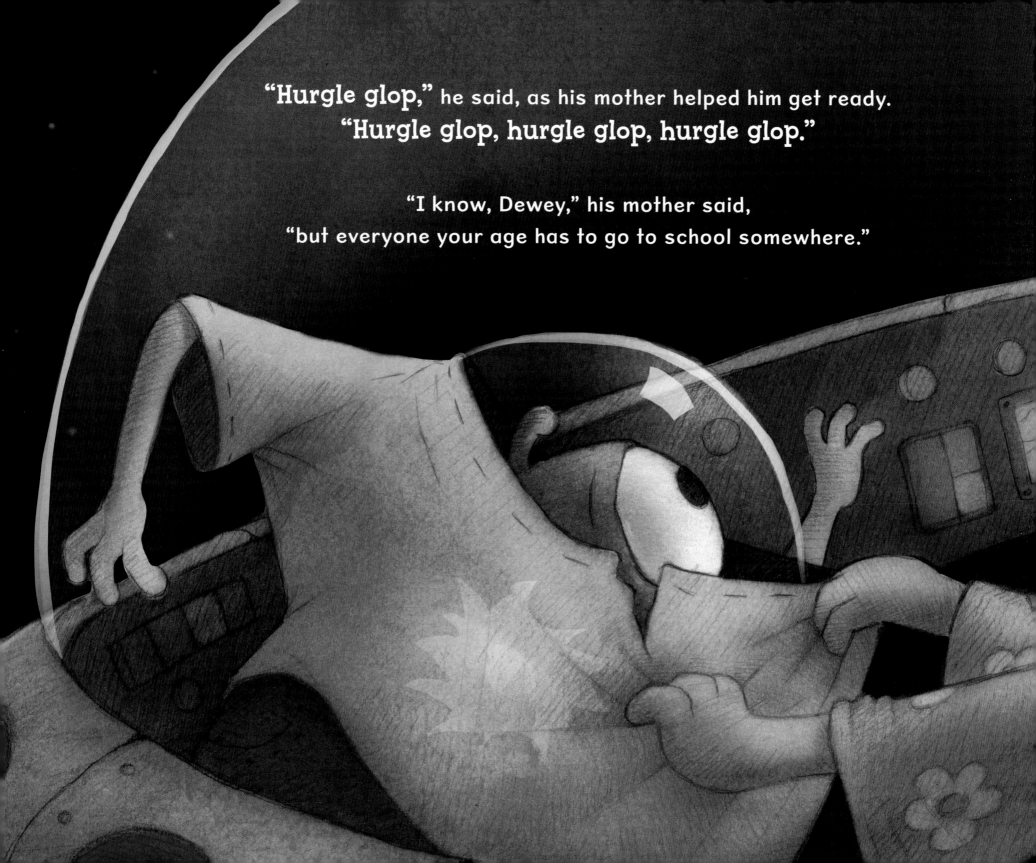

"Hurgle glop," he said, as his mother helped him get ready.
"Hurgle glop, hurgle glop, hurgle glop."

"I know, Dewey," his mother said,
"but everyone your age has to go to school somewhere."

So off they went.

Brand-new Earth shoes pinched his oofs.

Earth socks drooped around his hunklets.

Earth pants came way up over his urdle.

The *Ms. Brightsun's School for Little Learners* T-shirt he had to wear didn't fit him right in any direction and he felt like dorfling.

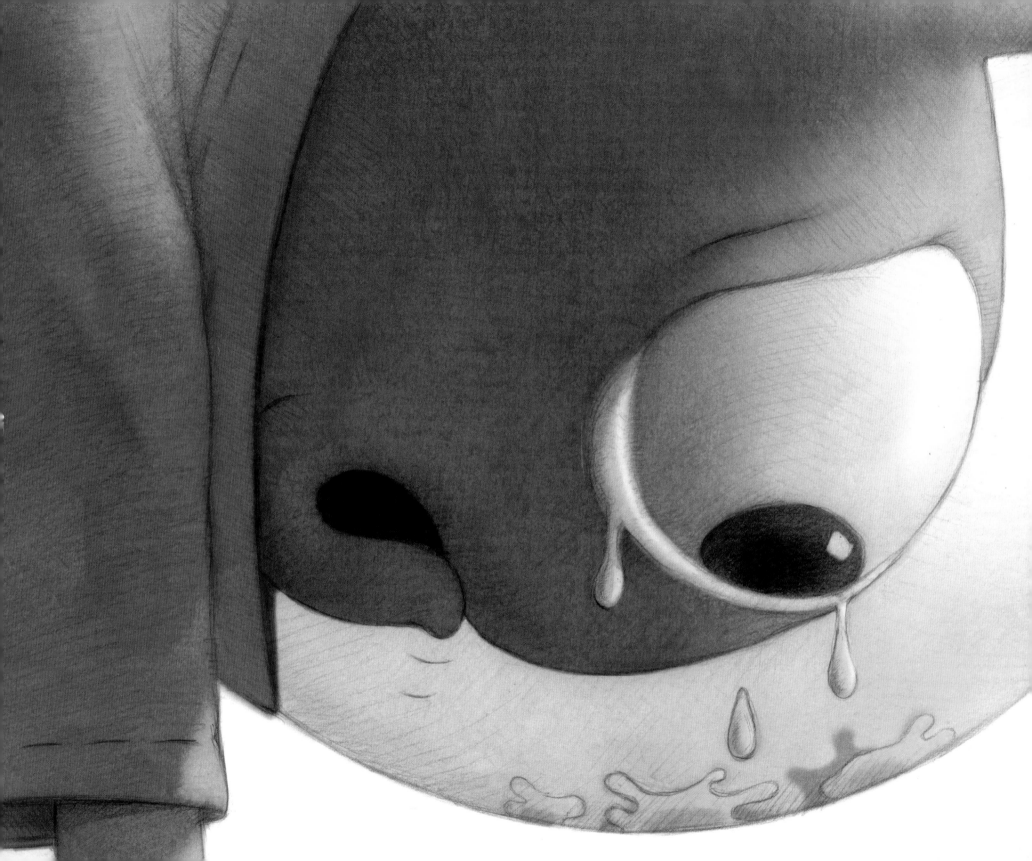

So even though he was pretty sure he was
much too old for it, he did. He dorfled.
Just a little, very quietly, all the way there.

Glop.

Glop.

Glop.

When they got to the open yellow doors
at *Ms. Brightsun's School*, Dewey's mother
dried his eye, kissed him on the eek,
and told him everything would be ootay.

But nothing was.

Ms. Brightsun's School was full of new things.
There were things called cubbies and things called books.
There was listening up and settling down and raising your
hand, not to mention his teacher, Ms. Brightsun,
who was ding, ding, dinging a shiny spaceship-shaped bell.

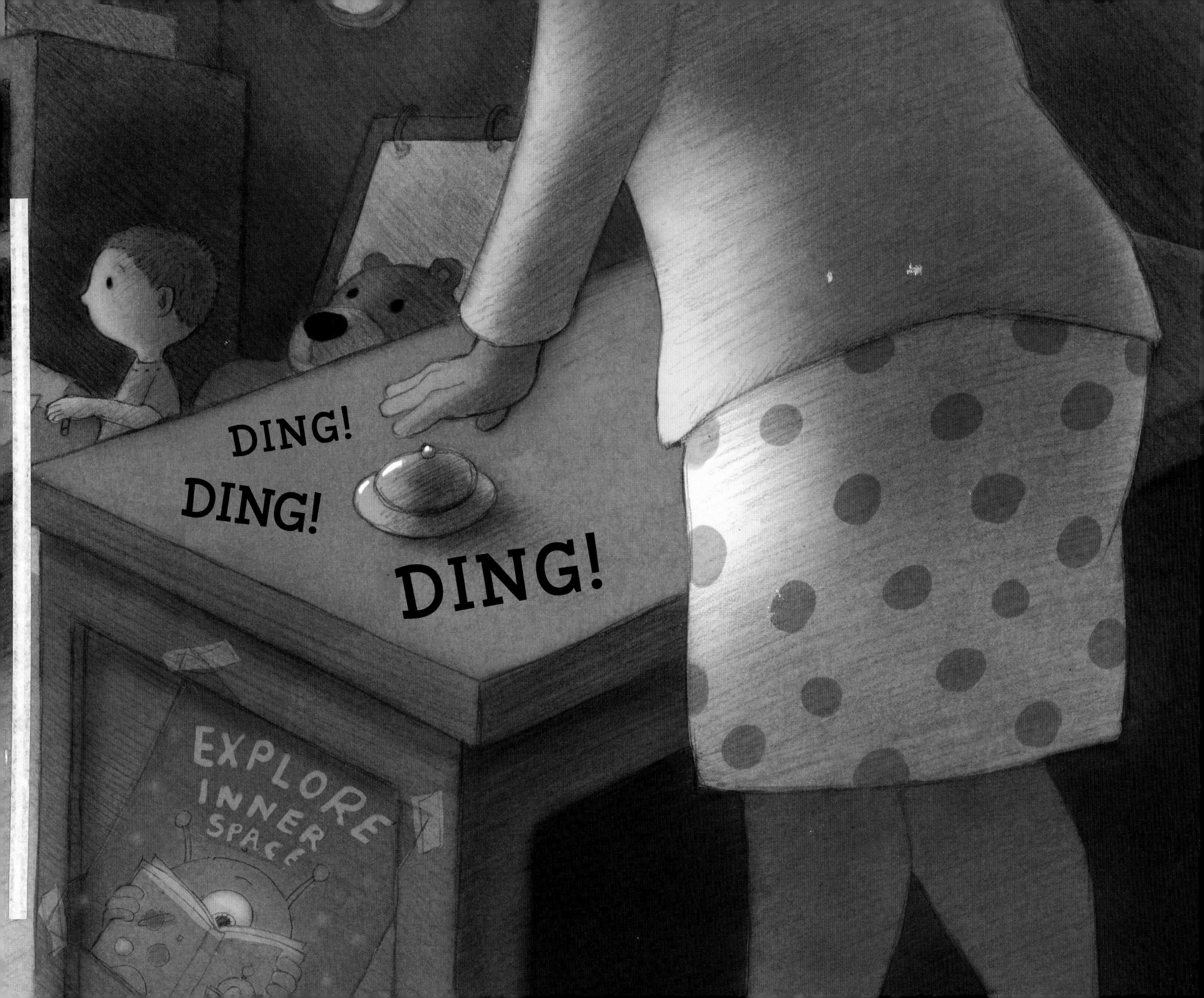

DING!

DING!

DING!

Earth noises sounded weird to Dewey's ears.

DING!
DING!
DING!

KOW?

Earth words felt
hard in his mouth.

Everything looked bright and strange and confusing . . .

Especially *Dewey.*

There were lots of kids in lots of different colors

but none of them were
Click-Clack Waddle-Waddle Dot-Dot Dewey Dew blue.

What they had two of,
he had one of.

What they had five of,
he had three of.

What they had lots of, he had none of.

When it was time to line up two-by-two for recess,
Click-Clack Waddle-Waddle Dot-Dot Dewey Dew
stood blue and confused at the back of the room,
with a tiny dorf threatening to squeeze up out of his eyeball.

But when **J.J. Burgdorf Havermeier the Third** smiled and said,
"Hi, my name is J.J., wanna stand in line with me?"

Click-Clack Waddle-Waddle Dot-Dot
Dewey Dew smiled back.

As they walked to the playground,
side by side, the light
from that smile grew so bright . . .

it sent a beam of happiness all the way
from *Ms. Brightsun's School,*

past the moons of Jupiter,

past **SPACE STATION ZOOMALOT,**

When Dewey's mother picked him up at the
end of the day, he told her all about playgrounds
and cubbies and **J.J. Havermeier the Third**.

Even though he was pretty sure he was
much too old for it, he let her pick him up and
spin him around and cover his eeks with kisses.

Because maybe, just maybe,
everything *was* going to be . . .

ootay.